This Little Tiger book belongs to:

_____

_____

_____

*For Dad*
~ C F

*For Andy, Caroline and Charlotte*
~ J C

LITTLE TIGER PRESS
1 The Coda Centre, 189 Munster Road, London SW6 6AW
www.littletiger.co.uk

First published in Great Britain 2004
This edition published 2016

Text copyright © Claire Freedman 2004
Illustrations copyright © Jane Chapman 2004
Visit Jane Chapman at www.ChapmanandWarnes.com
Claire Freedman and Jane Chapman have asserted their
rights to be identified as the author and illustrator of this
work under the Copyright, Designs and Patents Act, 1988

ISBN 978-1-84869-467-5
Printed in China
LTP/1900/1573/0616

2 4 6 8 10 9 7 5 3 1

# Dilly Duckling

Claire Freedman        Jane Chapman

**LITTLE TIGER PRESS**
London

One sunshiny day, the Ducks set off for a family waddle. Little Dilly was last in the line.

"Peekaboo!" Dilly said to the fish.
"Hello!" she called to the bugs
and dragonflies.

"Keep up, Dilly!" Mummy
Duck called. But Dilly was busy
watching a big blue butterfly.

She waddled after it when suddenly,
PUFF! a gust of wind blew out one
of her downy feathers!
   "Oh no!" gasped Dilly. "My feather!
It's flying away!"

Dilly raced after the big fluffy feather.

"Stop that feather!" she quacked loudly.

Wheeee!

The wind blew Dilly's downy feather this way
and that way . . . up in the air . . . and down again.

Round and round in circles ran Dilly dizzily, trying to catch it.

"Come back!" she called to her feather. But it floated further and further away.

Dilly flopped to the ground in a daze.
"What am I going to do?" she cried.
"Do about what?" asked Spike.
"My feather!" Dilly sighed. "It blew
away!"

"Was it yellow and fluffy?" Spike asked.
"Yes!" cried Dilly excitedly.
"It drifted down the hill!" Spike said.
"I'll get it!"

Spike curled himself into a tight ball.
He rolled downhill, spinning faster and faster.
"I'll try to spear your feather on my spikes!"
he shouted as he whizzed by.

"Wheeeeee!" Spike cried.
"Hooray!" quacked Dilly excitedly.

Bump! Spike landed in a hedge.
Puff! Up flew Dilly's feather again!
Slowly, Dilly's feather drifted down, down,
down, until it landed in a field.

Dilly and Spike pitter-pattered after it.

"It's caught on a corn stalk!" squeaked Nibble. "I'll get it for you!"

"Careful!" whispered Dilly.
"It's a very important feather!"

Nibble held her breath as she crept through the tall grass. Slowly she climbed the corn stalk. Gently she stretched out her paw . . .

"Atchoo!" sneezed Nibble as the feather tickled her twitchy nose! Wheeee! Off Dilly's feather flew.

The wind blew Dilly's feather up, up in the sky and far, far away.

"Sorry, Dilly!" Nibble called. "It's gone!"

"OH NO!" quacked Dilly, and she burst into tears.

"Oh, poor Dilly," said Spike.
"Don't cry!"
Nibble and Spike gave little
Dilly a 'cheer up' hug.

"I'll never see my fluffy feather again," Dilly sighed sadly. "I'm going home to tell my mummy."

Dilly waved her friends goodbye. "Thank you for trying to help me," she called.

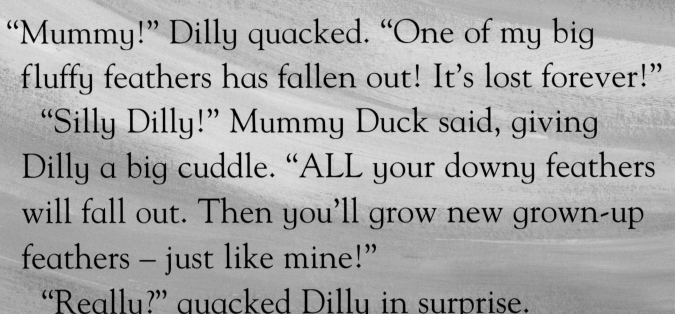

"Mummy!" Dilly quacked. "One of my big
fluffy feathers has fallen out! It's lost forever!"

"Silly Dilly!" Mummy Duck said, giving
Dilly a big cuddle. "ALL your downy feathers
will fall out. Then you'll grow new grown-up
feathers – just like mine!"

"Really?" quacked Dilly in surprise.
"So I'll look just like you!"

Dilly and Mummy Duck joined the
ducklings splashing in the river.
"Look!" Dilly cried. "There's my feather!"
"So it is!" said Mummy Duck.
"I don't need it any more, do I?" Dilly
giggled. "I'll grow another one!"
And quacking happily,
she dilly-dallied
off to play!